The River

Between

Times

James S. Wynecoop

Dedication

To my family for giving me the time and help in writing my stories.

James S. Wynecoop

Acknowledgment

To my brothers and sisters in Tribal Law Enforcement, who, along with me, learned the stories from our elders and ancestors.

About the Author

James S. Wynecoop began his public safety career in 1975 at the age of nineteen, becoming one of the youngest Tribal Police Officers on the Spokane Reservation. Those early years laid the foundation for a lifetime of service rooted in community, responsibility, and cultural heritage.

In 1985, Wynecoop traveled north to Alaska's North Slope, where he served as a Security Officer, Firefighter, and EMT in one of the most remote environments in the United States. Building on his experience, he founded Argus Security, a company that grew rapidly under his leadership—employing more than 500 security officers before being acquired in 1989.

Returning to law enforcement in 1990, Wynecoop accepted the position of Police Captain for the community of La Push, Washington. He later continued his federal service as a Police Officer with the U.S. Department of the Interior, Bureau of Indian Affairs, serving the North Idaho District and the Nez Perce Reservation until the position was eliminated by a reduction in force.

In 1999, Wynecoop joined the Kalispel Tribe of Indians to establish security operations for the Tribe's new casino. His leadership and vision propelled him into broader responsibility, and he was soon promoted to Executive Director of Public Safety. In this role, he oversaw the Police Department, Fire Department, and Emergency Medical Services, helping guide the growth of the Tribal community's modern public safety system.

After more than four decades in policing, security, fire, and emergency services, James S. Wynecoop retired in 2022—leaving behind a legacy of leadership, service, and commitment to Tribal communities across the Northwest and Alaska.

Table of Contents

Prologue

When The Water Remembers

Some rivers carve canyons.

Some carry salmon home.

Some wash away sins.

And some… remember.

Officer Jalen "Jay" Stormrunner had stood on the banks of the Iron River a hundred times, patrolling, thinking, praying, trying to understand his place in a world that never quite felt like it saw him. Part tribal, part not enough for some people, walking the line between two identities, two histories, two expectations.

But the night the river took him, it wasn't because he slipped.

It pulled him.

One breath, he was scanning for a missing fisherman—the next breath, he was standing in the early 1800s, watching smoke rise from a thriving Inland Salish village that no history book had ever shown him so clearly.

Children laughing.

Dogs weaving between lodges.

Warriors returning from the hunt.

Women crafting, cooking, living.

Alive. Whole. Unbroken.

Jay stood unseen in their world, the river's shimmer still clinging to him like cold light. Only one person sensed him—a young woman named Weyan, whose eyes caught the air where he stood, as if her spirit recognized what her sight could not.

Then the river took him back.

Since that night, both worlds began to unravel around him.

Sickness in the past.

A disturbance in the present.

A wanderer blowing a horn, only the old spirits understood.

And Jay—caught between times—forced to protect a people who should never have seen him.

But some destinies begin long before a man is born.

And some rivers are more than water.

Some rivers…are doors.

Chapter 1

When The River Took Him

Officer Jalen "Jay" Stormrunner didn't believe in portals, spirits, or anything that couldn't be logged in a police report.

Not until the night the river opened.

He was searching for a missing fisherman near Deadman's Bend, flashlight cutting through the fog, when a strange pulse rippled across the water. It wasn't light—wasn't electricity—more like the river exhaled.

Blue shimmer surged along the surface.

Jay stepped closer.

"Hello? Anyone there?"

The river brightened, humming like a struck tuning fork. The ground vibrated beneath his boots, pulling, tugging—

Then the world dropped.

A dazzling flash swallowed him whole, and the next breath he took was colder. Sharper. Older.

Jay staggered upright.

The modern road behind him was gone.

In its place rose towering pines thicker than power poles, bark dark with centuries. The river ran clearer, faster, untouched by dams or industry. Smoke drifted through the trees—woodsmoke, not exhaust.

And voices.

Salish words, soft and musical, floating on the breeze.

He followed the sound and stumbled into a thriving village: willow lodges, hide teepees, children laughing near the water, dogs weaving between them. Women scraped hides with stone tools; men carved bows, their hands swift and sure.

No one saw him.

He moved among them like a ghost.

Only one person reacted—a young woman named Weyan. She walked straight through him, shivering mid-step, hand rising to her cheek as though touched by winter air.

She whispered something to the elder beside her.

Before Jay could speak, a pulse rolled across the earth. The river shimmered again.

A second flash gripped him, yanking him backward—

And he landed face-first in mud on the modern bank.

But something remained in his hand.

A carved charm.

Old. Smooth. Sacred.

Jay stared at the river, heart pounding.

"What the hell was that?"

The river did not answer.

Chapter 2
The One Place The River Breathes Both Ways

Jay returned the next night.

Part hoping the river hadn't done what he remembered.

Part terrified it had.

By something he couldn't explain.

The water sensed him—shimmering at the edge like moonlight trapped beneath the surface. A hum vibrated in his bones. When he stepped closer, the glow reached for him.

He crossed again.

And again the village appeared.

Life unfolded around him—scraping hides, weaving baskets, children learning to fish with tiny bone hooks. Dogs barked at empty space when he passed, and children shivered as if brushed by a cold wind.

But only Weyan sensed him.

Each time she paused, eyes scanning the air, breath catching like she recognized a presence she couldn't quite see.

Back in the present, Jay sought the one person who might listen: Elder Mary-Two-Rivers.

He told her everything.

The flash.

The crossing.

The people.

The girl who sensed him.

She didn't blink.

Didn't laugh.

"The river remembers what time forgets," she said. "You were chosen."

Jay swallowed. "Why me?"

"Because someone must carry the warning."

"What warning?"

Her eyes saddened.

"You cannot stop what history brings. Disease. Missions. Children taken. But you can save those who must survive."

Jay whispered, "Who?"

"Ask the river."

That night, he knelt at the water's edge.

"Show me who I'm meant to save."

The river breathed—then pulled him under.

Chapter 3

The Shadow Begins To Take Form

He landed harder this time.

When he looked down, he saw it:

A shadow.

Faint. Flickering. But real.

A dog snarled at him, backing up with teeth bared. A child stopped mid-play, staring at the space Jay occupied. An elder muttered a word that made Jay's skin tingle.

"Shadow-walker."

Weyan stepped out of her lodge and froze.

She saw him.

Not clearly—but enough.

Her voice trembled.

"Are you here to warn us?"

Before Jay could answer, a horn blast echoed through the valley. Deep. Foreign. Wrong.

Jay knew the sound.

Fur traders.

The start of everything that would break this world.

He opened his mouth—

The river ripped him backward into darkness.

Chapter 4

Warnings Of What Must Come And What Can Be Saved

Modern lights stung his eyes as he stumbled onto the riverbank.

He tried telling fellow officers.

They thought he was cracking under stress.

He told his sergeant.

She suggested counseling.

So Jay went back to Elder Mary-Two-Rivers.

"You cannot stop the coming years," she told him. "Not the sickness. Not the missions. Not the removals."

Jay clenched his jaw.

"Then why show me anything?"

"Because you can save someone. Not all. But some. The river does not reveal without purpose."

Jay stared at the water.

"Who do I save?"

"Ask the river."

He touched the surface.

It answered.

Chapter 5

The First Sickness On the Wind

The world dissolved.

Jay opened his eyes in the early 1800s again—but this time the village was wrong.

Too quiet.

Too tense.

Too afraid.

Smoke hung low over the lodges. Dogs barked in uneasy bursts. Children clung to their mothers instead of playing by the river.

Then he heard it.

A cough.

Another.

A deep, rattling one that made his stomach drop.

Jay rushed to a lodge where a man lay trembling on furs, skin slick with fever. His wife whispered prayers, pressing a cloth to his head.

Jay examined him instinctively.

Fever.

Shallow breathing.

Discoloration around the lips.

Influenza.

Pneumonia.

Or much worse.

Weyan entered. She passed right through Jay, but shivered violently.

"Has he worsened?" she asked.

The woman nodded through tears.

Weyan felt the man's chest.

"The sickness is moving deeper."

Jay whispered, "She's right."

Another child appeared at the door.

"Weyan… another is sick."

The smell of sickness drifted across the camp on the wind.

Jay wanted to shout.

Wanted to warn them.

Wanted to help.

But he was still invisible.

Still powerless.

Weyan paused, sensing the cold pocket where he stood.

"Spirit," she whispered. "Tell us—what is coming?"

Jay lifted his hand toward her.

"I'm trying."

The river pulse slammed into him.

He was ripped backward into the modern world, collapsing on the riverbank.

Elder Mary-Two-Rivers waited.

"You saw it," she said softly.

Jay nodded, trembling.

"It's starting…"

She touched his shoulder.

"You cannot stop the storm. But you can shelter those meant to survive."

Jay whispered:

"I'll pay the price."

Chapter 6 When The Spirit Takes Form

Jay crossed again—and this time the village felt it.

Children pointed.

Dogs growled.

Mothers pulled little ones close.

His outline solidified—still shimmering, but visible.

A warrior stepped into the moonlight, eyes widening.

He could see Jay.

Before Jay could explain, the warrior lunged.

The spear pierced through Jay's chest—not entirely, not the way a weapon pierces flesh, but enough to tear his shirt and leave a trail of white steam curling from the wound.

But the blood…

The blood was real.

The warrior dropped the spear in horror.

Gasps rippled through the crowd.

"He bleeds!"

Weyan shoved her way through the circle, breath shaking. She reached out and touched his arm—

Her gasp echoed through the night.

"He is flesh."

Chaos erupted.

Some screamed.

Some prayed.

Some grabbed weapons.

Jay forced himself upright, chest burning.

"Get back!" he shouted. "Sickness is coming!"

He didn't explain.

Didn't have time.

"Not from me—it's from the outside—"

But the river seized him mid-sentence.

And he vanished.

Chapter 7 The First Time He Touches The Past

Cinematic Prose — Full Chapter

Jay hit the ground hard.

Not the soft, ghostlike landing from before.

This time, the impact punched the breath from his lungs.

Dust clung to his hands. His boots dug into the earth.

He was solid.

And the village knew it.

A shout tore across the clearing.

Jay rolled instinctively just as a spear sliced the air beside him.

Its stone tip tore straight through the sleeve of his jacket, ripping cloth and skin.

Pain flared—hot and entirely real.

He looked up to see Talek charging again, fury and fear mixed in equal measure.

Jay scrambled back, but Talek was fast—too fast.

The spear struck again, glancing off Jay's ribs, and bright red blood soaked into his shirt.

Gasps erupted around them.

"He bleeds!"

"He is no spirit!"

Jay staggered, vision blurring.

Weyan burst through the circle of warriors, voice sharp and desperate:

"Talek, stop! Look at him!"

Talek paused, breath ragged.

For the first time, uncertainty flickered in his eyes.

Weyan knelt beside Jay, gripping his arm.

Her voice shook.

"He is becoming real…"

Jay coughed hard, tasting copper. "It's happening," he managed. "I'm… changing."

Talek backed off a step—not out of fear, but out of awe.

The elder woman approached, leaning heavily on her staff.

Her eyes studied Jay with a knowing sadness.

"Two worlds," she whispered. "Two fires. And now the river gives you form."

Jay swallowed. "I'm not a spirit. I'm from another time."

The crowd murmured. Some frightened. Some curious.

Talek stepped forward.

"Another time? What does this mean?"

Jay wiped blood from his ribs.

"It means danger. Sickness. Strangers. Things that will destroy everything you know if you're not ready."

Weyan's breath hitched.

"Why did the river send you to us?"

Jay looked toward the young boy standing back near the lodge—the same boy who sensed him first, the one who seemed older than his years.

And Jay understood.

"I think I'm here to make sure someone survives," he said quietly.

The elder nodded slowly, as if she'd known all along.

The boy met Jay's gaze.

And the river's purpose deepened.

Chapter 8 The First Lessons

The next morning, Jay woke to the low thrum of drums.

Sweat lodge preparations.

He followed the sound to the edge of the village, where men bent willow branches into a dome, covering the frame with elk hides. Stones heated red-hot in a nearby fire.

The air smelled of cedar and sage and something older than time.

An elderly woman approached him.

"You carry two fires," she murmured.

"One from the ancestors behind you…

One from the world ahead."

She touched his chest lightly, as though feeling the heartbeat of both worlds within him.

Jay couldn't find words.

Inside the sweat lodge, the men sang. Their voices vibrated through the earth, through Jay's bones, through the river that bound their worlds. He knelt outside, head bowed.

He whispered a Christian prayer—not to replace theirs, but to walk beside it.

A strange peace settled over him.

A bridge between two ways of believing.

When the men emerged, steam rising from their skin, Weyan hurried over.

"Come," she said. "The sick man is failing."

Jay followed her to the lodge of the first patient.

The man's breathing was wet and labored.

His skin had gone pale beneath the fever.

His wife looked at Jay with desperate eyes—even though she still wasn't sure if he was a man or a spirit.

Jay knelt beside the bed of furs.

"You must boil your water," he said. "Separate anyone who is sick. Clean every tool with hot water. Burn blankets he has used."

A hunter frowned. "This is not our way."

"It is the only way to slow the sickness," Jay said firmly. "If you don't, more will fall ill."

Weyan backed him.

"This spirit-man knows things we do not. Let him try."

The elder woman nodded.

Jay demonstrated everything he knew—washing his hands, boiling clothes, and cleaning tools. Slowly, suspicion gave way to quiet hope.

The young boy stood in the doorway watching.

Silent.

Studying every movement.

Weyan leaned close and whispered,

"That boy… he dreams of things before they happen. The elders believe the river speaks to him."

Jay looked at the boy and felt the weight of destiny settle on his shoulders.

"He's important," Jay whispered. "For the future that's coming."

Weyan nodded.

"Then we will protect him."

Chapter 9 The Man Who Walks Two Worlds

Days passed.

Jay no longer floated through the village like a ghost—he worked alongside them.

He carried firewood.

Fetched water.

Checked on the sick.

Sat with elders and listened to stories older than his entire world.

Children trailed after him everywhere he went, whispering "shadow-man" or "river-man" before giggling and hiding behind each other.

Talek watched him carefully at first, arms crossed, jaw clenched.

But slowly, suspicion softened.

"You stand between us and danger," Talek said one evening. "A man does not have to be born here to be one of us."

Jay smiled faintly. "I see the strength of your people."

Later, as the sun bled orange across the sky, the elder woman called Jay to sit beside her.

"In the old days," she began, "there was a man who carried two fires. One fire burned for the world behind him—his childhood, his teachings. The other fire burned for the world ahead—what he had yet to become."

Jay listened, heart tight.

"The man had to choose which fire to follow," she continued. "If he chose wrong, the people suffered."

Jay swallowed.

"And if he chose right?"

"Then the world lived."

Jay looked toward the boy.

Small.

Quiet.

Watching him with eyes far older than his years.

"He is the one I must protect," Jay said quietly.

The elder smiled sadly.

"Yes. The river has told us the same."

Chapter 10 When The Outside World Arrives

Iron River Bend — The First Collision of Two Worlds

Jay had been sure of one thing that morning—before he had even opened his eyes in the past.

The day had started wrong.

The air had been too still. The birds were too scattered. The dogs are pacing in short circles around the lodges. Even the river felt different—slower in its breathing, like it knew to wait for something.

He had not been here by accident.

Something was coming.

Jay found people parting for him as he walked through the camp. Not many… but more than before. Women pressed fingertips to their lips when they caught his eye, whispering prayers. Children watched his shadow with the same sense of dread they reserved for snakes in the grass. Talek, the warrior who had once tried to spear him, nodded respectfully.

Jay had become real enough to fear—and real enough to trust.

Weyan found Jay at the edge of the morning fire, her hair braided with the first signs of autumn feathers.

"You feel it too," she said.

Jay nodded.

"Something's wrong."

Before she could answer, two sharp whistle blasts cut through the air—two notes from the hilltop lookout.

Talek strode purposefully out from the lodge, spear in hand.

"Strangers on the river," he growled. "Big canoes. Three, maybe four."

Jay felt his pulse thicken.

The traders.

The moment Jay had been waiting for, dreading, since the river had first dragged him into this life.

Men with rifles.

Men who brought blankets washed with sickness.

Men who smiled while they broke nations.

Jay took his place beside Talek and the warriors on the bluff above the river bend. From here, he could see them—long dark canoes cutting through the water like iron blades. Men in heavy coats, wide-brimmed hats, bright sashes. A flag at the bow of one of the canoes—flapping empty white paint and bright red line in the breeze as if the man in the front wanted to announce his peaceful intentions with cloth alone.

Jay knew better.

Weyan stepped beside him, her eyes narrowing.

"I have seen men like these before," she whispered. "They take more than they give."

Jay exhaled slowly.

"They bring weapons, goods… and danger none of you can see yet."

Talek glanced at Jay with an unreadable expression.

"Will they see you as we do?" he asked.

Jay swallowed.

"I don't know."

Because each time the river brought Jay back… the rules changed.

A second whistle cut through the pines—three notes this time.

The alarm for preparation, not flee.

Families herded children away from the river, toward the shelter of the lodges. Women pulled drying racks of salmon into the safety of their homes. Dogs were tied closely. Elders shuffled into the shadows. Warriors took positions at the edge of the riverbank in layers—standard procedure for a first approach.

Weyan tightened the wrap around her shoulders.

"They will try to give gifts first," she murmured. "To get us close. To make us trust."

Jay nodded grimly.

"Blankets. Cloth. Beads. And maybe whiskey."

Talek's head whipped around to Jay.

"What is whiskey?"

"A drink," Jay said, "that destroys villages."

Talek's jaw clenched like carved stone.

"Then none of it enters this camp."

The canoes scraped the gravel with a slow, gritty sound.

The traders spilled out, boots caking in the mud.

Jay stood behind the warriors, trying to breathe normally—trying not to shake. If they saw him, it would change everything. If they didn't, he might move unseen. Either way, today mattered.

The man in front—tall, sharp-eyed, exuding confidence—stepped forward with both hands raised.

"Good day to you!" he boomed in English, then repeated with ungainly motions in Chinuk Wawa.

Talek said nothing. He did not need to.

Weyan leaned toward Jay without looking at him:

"Say nothing. Let our people speak first."

Jay nodded.

The head trader plastered a wide smile on his face that did not reach his eyes.

"We come for good trade! Good blankets! Good steel! Fair deals for friends!"

Talek finally stepped forward, spear planted in the gravel.

"You stand at the edge of our land," he said in firm Salish. "Say your names and your purpose."

The translator repeated it.

The trader puffed out his chest.

"Jean-Louis Marquette, Montréal Company."

Jay froze.

Marquette.

He knew that name—from tribal records, from stories passed by elders, from the lists of which traders had caused trouble long before treaties were forced.

This man's return was a single thread that could unravel decades.

Jay's stomach churned.

Marquette gestured to the crates at the bottom of his canoe.

"We bring gifts to show good faith!"

Weyan leaned toward Jay, barely.

"Gifts," she repeated bitterly. "Gifts that bind us in debt."

She was right.

Jay leaned toward her in turn.

"They expect loyalty. And payment ten times what the gifts are worth."

Talek motioned for quiet as the translator reached to open the crate.

Shiny metal knives and kettles.

Beads.

Awls.

And under it all—

Red cloth blankets.

Fresh.

Folded.

Contaminated.

Jay stiffened, breath going ragged.

Talek saw his reaction.

"What is it?"

"Blankets," Jay said quietly. "They're dangerous."

Weyan's eyes flicked to him.

"Dangerous how?"

Jay forced the words out.

"There are sicknesses—diseases—you do not know. They travel in cloth. The traders don't always know they carry it."

Talek didn't hesitate.

He stepped between the crate and the other men.

"No blankets."

The translator translated.

Marquette blinked, offended.

"No blankets? Everyone wants blankets."

Talek repeated, louder:

"No blankets."

But Marquette wasn't finished.

Jay saw the bottle coming before Marquette even took it out.

Whiskey.

Amber gold in the sunlight.

"Fine drink!" Marquette said brightly. "Warms the heart. Traders everywhere enjoy!"

Jay's heartbeat kicked.

He found himself stepping beside Talek without thinking.

"No drink," Jay said.

Talek had his back immediately.

"No drink," he echoed.

Marquette blinked.

"You don't take blankets. You don't take a drink. What do you take?"

Talek lifted his chin.

"What keeps our children alive?"

The translator nodded reluctantly.

Marquette didn't hide his disappointment this time.

He shut the crate with a crack.

"Then the trade is small today," he said flatly.

But Jay saw the moment Marquette's eyes slid past Talek—

past Weyan—

past the warriors and elders—

toward the boy standing close to the water's edge.

The boy who didn't yet understand the danger.

The boy Jay knew he had to protect.

The boy who mattered to the future in ways the river had not yet revealed.

Marquette took one casual step forward.

Jay felt something snap inside him.

He moved, shoving himself right in front of the trader and the child.

Marquette stopped, eyebrows going up.

Jay's voice was low and hard.

"No."

Talek immediately moved to Jay's side, the spear across his body.

Weyan was behind the boy in an instant, gently pushing him away.

Marquette raised both hands.

"Very well," he said quietly. "Trade only."

But he was still staring at Jay.

Too curious.

Too calculating.

As Jay watched him, a weight settled in his chest—the feeling that today had only just begun.

Outside forces had found the village.

And they would be back.

And every time the river took Jay home…

He would return to a world that was slowly, inevitably, changing.

Chapter 11 When Trade Comes With Teeth

Cinematic Prose — Full Rewrite to Fit the Story

The river had warned them.

The air had the same uneasy electricity as the nights before, as if the world knew something sharp was coming. Jay could feel it as soon as he crossed. The village was restless, the warriors keyed up, and the mothers held their children closer for reasons they couldn't even name.

Scouts came back by midday, breathless.

"Strangers," one wheezed. "Paddling upstream. Three men. Rifles. Cloth with strange colors."

Jay's stomach dropped.

The first ones.

The ones history had etched warnings about in every elder's caution and every tribal council record.

Talek shouted orders.

Women pulled their children behind the lodge barriers.

The elders watched the river like it had become a mouth opening to swallow something sacred.

Jay stood with the warriors, heart banging in his chest.

Would the traders see him?

Would the river hide him?

Or had he crossed too many times to stay unseen?

Jay would find out the moment the canoes scuffed the gravel.

The lead trader—a big man, well-fed, coat with fur trim—stepped into the shallows, and his eyes snagged on Jay immediately.

No confusion.

No pause.

Recognition.

"Oh," he said, in a butchered English, "a man who looks like one of you… But it is not."

Jay's jaw clenched.

Weyan pressed to his side, whispering in Salish, "Do not speak first. They must not think you are their voice."

Talek moved to the front, spear poised.

"You are on our land," he said icily. "Say your names."

The trader bopped his chest.

"Jean-Louis Marquette," he announced. "We have fine trade. Blankets. Rifles. Tools. Gifts for friends."

Gifts.

Jay nearly laughed.

Gifts were the first hook.

Debt came after.

Dependence came next.

And sickness was carried on the backs of those red-trimmed blankets.

Jay raised his voice.

"No blankets."

Every head turned.

A hunter leaned in, whispering, "He dares speak across clans…"

Talek seemed startled—but only for a moment.

He trusted Jay now, even if he didn't know why.

"No blankets," Talek said again. "Your clothes stay on your boats."

Marquette blinked. "Why? It is beautiful! Warm! Perfect for children."

Jay stepped forward, eyes boring into Marquette.

"They come from another camp," Jay said. "A camp with sickness."

A ripple of fear went through the warriors.

Marquette's smile wavered for a heartbeat.

Then he laughed it off.

"Very well," he said lightly. "No blankets. But you will like this."

He raised a glass bottle, amber liquid catching the sunlight.

Jay stiffened.

Whiskey.

Talek didn't recognize it—but Weyan did.

She'd heard the elders talk of poison-water from old memories of raids on the coastal tribes.

Jay spoke before Talek could.

"No drink," Jay said sharply. "Not a drop."

Talek echoed him without thought.

"No drink."

Marquette frowned. "You want nothing?"

"We want no danger," Weyan said, steady.

Marquette shrugged, hands in the air.

"Then trade is… less good."

"Trade should be clean," Talek said.

The tension lessened—just a little—until Marquette's eyes strayed from them.

To the boy.

Small.

Quiet.

Watching with those deep, ancient eyes.

The trader softened his expression, squatting a little lower.

"Bonjour, petit," he said. "Come. See pretty beads."

The boy hesitated.

Jay didn't.

He stepped forward, cutting the path completely.

"Stay away from him," Jay said.

Not loud.

Not aggressive.

But with an edge that cut.

Marquette blinked. "I mean no harm."

"You do not come near the children."

Jay didn't move. Didn't blink.

Talek joined him, spear lowered but poised.

"No child of our people comes near you," Talek said.

The translator—a Native man in a mishmash of trade gear—swallowed hard.

"They mean this with sincerity," he said to Marquette in French.

Marquette straightened, hands up in mock surrender.

"Very well," he said. "We trade tools only."

But the warmth in his smile had gone brittle.

Cold.

Calculating.

The river behind Jay thrummed softly, like a heartbeat warning him to pay attention.

Weyan leaned in close.

"You guarded him… with more fear than when the spear struck you."

Jay's throat tightened.

"That boy… is tied to the future. If anything happens to him, the world you know… the world I come from… changes forever."

Weyan's breath caught.

Talek's grip tightened on his spear.

The elder woman's voice echoed in Jay's memory:

Protect the boy. Protect the girl who sees you. Protect the warrior who doubts you.

The river had not sent Jay back only to watch history unfold.

It had sent him to change it.

But Marquette's eyes—calculating, hungry—told Jay the man would return.

And next time, he wouldn't bring gifts.

He'd bring teeth.

Chapter 12 The Shadow In The Timber

The forest was too quiet.

Jay felt it before he heard anything, like a pressure in his ears, a faint hum inside the bones of the land. The same woods that usually rang with birdsong and distant woodpeckers now held a stillness so heavy it felt alive.

He wasn't alone.

He knew it the way animals know a coming storm.

Jay tightened the leather cord around his wrist—the one Weyan had given him to anchor him in this world—then stepped deeper into the pines, following that instinctual pull.

The boy was missing.

Talek had gone to check the far hunting trail. Weyan was gathering the women in the village to keep the children close. But Jay… Jay had seen the river's vision. He saw the boy screaming in the trees, a shadow dragging him backward.

And that vision didn't wait.

Jay wasn't waiting either.

The forest thickened, pine needles muffling his steps. He scanned the forest floor—nothing human, just small prints from deer and foxes, and the soft, dragging marks left by wind-blown branches.

But something else was there, too.

A partial footprint pressed at an angle.

Too deep.

Too narrow.

Too long.

Jay crouched and brushed the dirt with his fingers.

Not an animal.

Not a villager.

Not a trader.

Something walking upright…

But wrong.

The chill snaked up his spine.

He followed the print deeper into the woods toward the ridge where yesterday's smoke signal had appeared. The trees grew tighter, tall pines leaning over the path like guardians warning him away.

Ahead, the air changed. Cold, like a breath.

Jay stopped.

Something stood between the trees.

Not fully formed—not dissolved either.

A shape.

A shadow.

A suggestion of a figure, tall and thin, with edges that wavered like heat on stone.

Jay's heart pounded, but he stepped forward.

"Who are you?" he called.

The shadow didn't move.

Jay felt the river pulse faintly behind his ribs. Not calling him home—warning him.

"Are you following me?" he pushed. "Why?"

The shape twitched, as if reacting to his voice. Jay's hand drifted toward the obsidian blade Weyan had given him—not a weapon he knew well, but solid enough to give courage.

The forest inhaled.

Then, the shadow stepped back into the trees and vanished.

Jay released a shaky breath.

Whatever it was, it wasn't aimless. It was watching him intentionally.

He turned to leave—

—and nearly collided with Talek.

The Hunter's Warning

Talek's chest heaved with exertion, his hair damp with sweat.

"You saw it," he said without question.

Jay nodded slowly.

"What is it?" Jay asked.

Talek stared hard into the timber.

"A wanderer," he said. "Or a spirit. Or something that once was man."

Jay frowned. "You've seen it before?"

Talek hesitated.

"Only once," he admitted. "I was a boy. It stood outside my father's lodge after my uncle disturbed a grave." His jaw tightened. "My uncle died three nights later."

Jay's blood chilled. "You think it's tied to the graves here?"

"I think," Talek answered, "that something was disturbed. And it follows the scent of the one who can see between worlds."

Jay felt the weight of that hit him square in the chest.

"You think it's after me."

"I do not think," Talek said sharply. "I know."

The forest moaned with a shifting gust of wind.

"We must go back," Talek added. "Weyan said the boy is missing."

Jay's stomach dropped.

The boy.

The one the river showed screaming.

"Then we don't waste time," Jay said.

He moved first, Talek matching pace beside him, both sprinting back toward the village. Pine branches whipped against Jay's arms, and breath burned his lungs, but he pushed harder—

—because fear was already well ahead of him.

The Missing Boy

They reached the village breathless. Weyan ran toward them at once.

"He's gone," she said, voice tight with fear. "The boy. His mother thought he went to wash his hands. He never came back."

"Tracks?" Jay asked.

Talek nodded. "Leading north."

Jay didn't hesitate.

Weyan grabbed his arm. "Jay—don't go alone."

He met her gaze. "Then come with me."

She let out a breath between fear and determination.

"We will all go," she said. "This is our child."

Jay nodded once.

Talek gathered two hunters.

Birch-Woman stepped from the lodge, chanting under her breath.

Weyan armed herself with a bone-handled knife.

Together they moved into the forest.

Jay felt the ripple of time humming inside him—like the river was tightening its grip, like the future was balancing on a thin, fragile thread.

The boy's life.

Something had taken him.

Something old.

Something without memory.

Something the wanderer's horn had tried to warn against.

Jay stopped suddenly.

A distant cry carried through the trees.

Weyan froze. "Was that—?"

Jay nodded, pulse racing. "Yes."

They bolted toward the sound.

Branches snapped.

Leaves trembled.

Voices echoed as the group split wider to cover more ground.

Jay charged ahead until he reached a narrow clearing.

And there—

At the far end—

A small figure lay on the ground, trembling, hands over his ears.

The boy.

Jay sprinted forward, dropping to his knees beside him.

"It's okay," Jay whispered. "I've got you."

The boy's eyes were wide with terror. "It was following me," he whimpered. "It had no face."

Weyan caught up, dropping beside them, pulling the boy into her arms.

"What happened?" she breathed.

The boy pointed shakily toward the trees.

"There."

Jay followed his gaze.

The shadow stood at the forest edge.

Still.

Watching.

For the first time, Jay saw its shape clearly.

It wasn't tall anymore—not human-shaped.

It bent wrong.

As if memory itself had tried to rebuild a man and failed.

Jay rose slowly.

"Why are you after him?" he demanded.

The shadow tilted its head.

Jay felt something push against his chest—an icy wave of emotion.

Not anger.

Not hunger.

Sorrow.

Deep, endless sorrow.

Weyan whispered, trembling, "Jay—don't go closer."

But he did.

Because the river had chosen him.

Because some things you only learn by stepping into the dark.

Jay lowered his obsidian blade.

"I'm not here to hurt you," he said softly. "But you can't have him."

The shadow wavered.

Then—

A horn call echoed through the trees.

The wanderer's horn.

Low.

Ancient.

Commanding.

The shadow convulsed—then dissolved like smoke in the wind.

Gone.

Jay exhaled shakily.

Talek and the hunters burst into the clearing moments later, weapons ready.

But it was over.

Weyan pressed the boy's face into her shoulder, tears streaking her cheeks.

Jay stood staring at the place where the shadow had vanished.

And he knew one thing:

This was not the end.

It was the beginning.

Chapter 13 When The River Pulls Him Back

The boy wouldn't let go of Jay's shirt.

Even after the shadow disappeared and the horn's echo faded, those small fingers remained knotted in the fabric like he was afraid Jay would dissolve too.

"It's gone," Weyan whispered, voice quivering. "It's gone, little one. You're safe."

The boy didn't reply. His eyes remained fixed on the trees where the shadow had been.

Jay squeezed his shoulder gently. "Can you talk to me?" he asked. "Tell me what you saw?"

The boy's lips trembled.

"It… tried to pull my eyes out," he whispered.

Weyan sucked in a breath.

Jay shook his head. "No. Not your eyes," he said softly. "It wanted something inside them. What you see. What you dream."

The boy flinched like Jay had confirmed his worst fear.

Talek approached slowly, spear lowered now, eyes scanning the treeline. "We should get him back to the village," he said. "Whatever that was, it may not be the only one."

Birch-Woman arrived last, leaning on her carved staff. Her face had grown even more lined in the short time they'd been gone.

"You felt it, didn't you?" she asked Jay.

"Yeah," he answered. "It wasn't just… evil."

"No," she agreed. "It is not evil. It is broken. That makes it worse."

The boy shifted closer to Weyan, clutching her skirt.

"Broken how?" Jay asked.

Before Birch-Woman could answer, Jay felt something inside his ribs twist.

The river.

He knew the sensation now—the way the world seemed to suck in a breath, the way his heartbeat fell out of rhythm with his own body. The pull of the water wasn't physical; it was like someone grabbing the loose edge of his soul.

"Not now," he muttered.

His vision blurred.

Weyan saw his posture change. "Jay?" she asked quickly. "What's happening?"

He opened his mouth to answer, but his voice came out hollow.

"The river," he whispered. "It's—"

The world snapped.

Trees vanished.

Voices cut off.

The ground dropped.

He was jerked backward by something no one else could see.

The last thing he heard was the boy crying out, "Don't let him go!"

Then white.

Cold.

Impact.

Back to 1984

Jay hit the gravel bar on the modern bank so hard his shoulder exploded in pain. He rolled instinctively, training taking over, trying to distribute the impact instead of letting it break him.

It didn't work.

A rock caught him just below the ribs, and for a moment he could only wheeze, lungs refusing to pull in air.

The river roared beside him, innocent as ever.

"When I said I'd pay the price," he gasped to the sky, "I didn't mean all at once."

A distant engine hummed somewhere up on the highway. The smell of exhaust faintly mixed with pine.

He pushed himself upright, teeth clenched, hand pressed to his side. His shirt was torn where Talek's spear had once passed through him—another time, another world—but the bruise underneath was new, blooming angry and deep.

Two worlds.

One body.

He fumbled for his radio.

"Dispatch… 24," he croaked.

Nothing.

The radio crackled, hissed, then went dead again.

The river wasn't interested in giving him help today.

Jay sat back on his heels, breathing carefully, and looked at the water.

"You pulled me out right when they needed me," he said, anger simmering under the pain. "Why?"

The river said nothing.

But the current shifted, just slightly. A small whirlpool formed near the bend, spinning in place like a finger drawing a circle in the air.

Jay stared at it.

"Did I break something?" he asked quietly. "By stopping the traders' blankets? By keeping the boy safe? Is this about changing the future?"

The river kept moving, indifferent and relentless.

Something in his peripheral vision caught his attention. Across from the gravel bar, on the modern far bank, a patch of land looked… wrong.

Fresh dirt.

Exposed roots.

The kind of scar the earth wears when something has been dug up in a hurry.

Jay frowned.

This wasn't just a time ripple. This was real. Now.

He squinted.

The disturbed patch sat just above the high-water mark, not far from where he knew—knew in his bones—an old burial ground had once been, long before the agency put up signs, long before half the graves were washed away by erosion.

"Graves," he whispered.

The shadow.

The wanderer.

The horn.

The pieces were starting to float toward each other, not yet fitting, but refusing to stay apart.

He forced himself to stand, shoulder screaming.

If someone was disturbing graves now—in his time—it might be tied to everything happening in theirs.

The Split Responsibilities

Back at the Agency offices, the lights buzzed with their usual tired electrical hum. The old coffee maker burbled in the corner, burning the last half pot into something that smelled like battery acid.

Jay walked in stiffly, trying not to show how much every step hurt.

His sergeant, Lisa Harper, looked up from a stack of reports.

"Stormrunner, you look like you got in a fight with a logging truck," she said.

"Rock," he answered. "Won."

She raised an eyebrow. "Need a medic?"

"Had one," he muttered, thinking of Weyan's hands, the elder's herbs, another world's remedies. "I'm fine."

She didn't buy it, but she let it go.

"We've had some calls about kids messing around near the old river burial sites," she said instead. "Somebody thought they heard digging at night. You want it?"

Jay's pulse ticked up.

"Yeah," he said. "I want it."

"Take it easy," she warned. "Last thing we need is you chasing ghost stories when we're short-staffed."

If you only knew, he thought.

He took the file from her and flipped it open. Photos. Complaints. Not much, but enough to triangulate the area.

Same ridge.

Same bend.

Old graves.

Something was definitely wrong.

Yanked Again

Jay drove back to the bend as the sky slipped toward evening, shadows stretching long over the river. He parked the patrol unit in the turnout, grabbed a flashlight and camera out of habit, and walked down the trail.

His shoulder throbbed, but he ignored it.

As he approached the water, the shimmer started— subtle at first, like heat rising from asphalt. The hair on his arms lifted.

"Not yet," he warned the river. "I've got something to check first."

It shimmered brighter in response.

"Of course, you do," he muttered.

He crossed to the opposite side using the old footbridge farther upstream, then walked back along the bank until he reached the disturbed patch he'd seen from the other side.

Up close, it was worse.

Someone had dug a long, narrow trench and then sloppily tried to cover it.

Not an animal.

Not erosion.

A shovel.

He crouched, pressing fingers into the loose soil.

Pieces of broken bone lay half-buried, pale against the dark dirt.

Human.

Jay's jaw clenched.

"Whoever did this," he said quietly, "brought that thing back."

The river hummed.

The air grew thinner, like he was at the top of a mountain.

He stood and looked toward the water.

"All right," he said. "You want me back over there? Fine. But you're going to start answering questions."

As if on cue, the shimmer intensified, stretching across the current like a pale curtain.

Jay took one breath, then another, braced himself—

—and stepped into the light.

The world spun.

His wounded shoulder screamed.

Voices rose around him—

—and he dropped hard into the past.

Back Too Late

He hit dirt instead of stone this time. Someone rolled him onto his back before he'd fully processed where—or when—he was.

"Jay! Jay!"

Weyan's voice.

He blinked.

Her face came into focus above him, eyes wide, hair half-unbound, breath ragged like she'd been running.

"You left," she said, equal parts accusation and relief. "You were there—and then you were not."

"I didn't have much of a choice," he groaned, trying to sit up. "The river—"

"We know," Talek cut in, standing just behind her. "It took you. But it took more than that."

Jay's stomach dropped.

"What?"

Talek's jaw clenched.

"The boy," Weyan whispered. "Since you vanished, he has not spoken. He will not eat. He only stares toward the trees, like he is listening to something only he can hear."

Jay forced himself up, every muscle protesting.

"Take me to him," he said.

They led him back to the village.

Children usually raced past, kicking sticks, chasing dogs, playing make-believe wars. Today they watched from doorways and behind their mothers' skirts, eyes big and solemn.

The boy sat on a log near the edge of camp, looking toward the timber where the shadow had appeared. His hands rested limp on his knees. His face had lost its softness; even in stillness, there was a strange tension in it, as if something inside was coiled.

Jay approached slowly, kneeling in front of him.

"Hey," he said softly. "You remember me?"

No answer.

The boy's eyes barely flicked toward him.

"Do you remember what happened?" Jay tried again. "In the trees? With the shadow?"

The boy's lips parted, but no sound came out.

Weyan's hand came to rest on Jay's shoulder.

"It is as if part of him stayed out there," she whispered.

Jay swallowed.

Or part of it stayed in him.

He reached out carefully, touching two fingers to the boy's wrist.

Cold shot up his arm.

Not physical cold—worse. A sense of being watched from inside the boy, as if something peered through his eyes and weighed Jay in silence.

Jay didn't flinch.

"I don't know what you are," he said very quietly, addressing not the boy, but the thing. "But you're not staying."

The boy blinked once, slow, like he'd just emerged from underwater.

"Did you… hear that?" he whispered.

Jay's breath hitched.

"Hear what?"

"The horn," the boy said. "It… calls to it."

Weyan stiffened. "The wanderer's horn?"

The boy shook his head.

"No," he whispered, eyes going distant again. "The one… that isn't his."

Jay's veins turned to ice.

There were two calls now.

The wanderer's horn that tried to send the spirit away—

And another that called it back.

"Who blows the other one?" Jay asked, voice barely above a breath.

The boy's gaze slid toward the ridge.

"In the trees," he said. "Where the smoke rises."

Birch-Woman's warning echoed in Jay's mind.

The smoke speaks.

The threads of the world shift.

He stood slowly, looking from Weyan to Talek to the boy.

"I have to talk to someone," he said.

"Who?" Weyan asked.

"An old man," Jay answered. "In my world."

"Why?" Talek frowned.

"Because he's seen this too," Jay said. "Or something like it. And if I'm going to keep your boy alive…"

He glanced back toward the river, already feeling its pull.

"…I need every story anyone ever told about horns, graves, and things that don't belong to either world."

The river shimmered faintly in his peripheral vision.

It had yanked him away once without warning.

This time, he'd go willingly.

He laid a hand briefly on the boy's shoulder.

"I'll be back," he said.

The boy finally met his eyes fully.

"You always say that," the boy murmured. "I hope it stays true."

Jay swallowed against the lump in his throat.

"Me too, little man," he said softly. "Me too."

The river called.

He answered.

Chapter 14 The Echo In The Trees

Jay walked home long after the shimmer had dropped him back into 1984.

The patrol unit sat alone at the turnout, dew beginning to gather on its hood. The sky was fully dark now, stars hiding behind a thick ceiling of cloud. Only the faint orange glow from a town far off painted the horizon.

He shut the unit door gently, not ready for the sound of civilization yet, and cut through the trees instead of taking the gravel road.

The forest at night on the reservation had always been a strange comfort. As a boy, he'd walked it with his grandfather, learning which animal calls meant curiosity and which meant get the hell out now. As a cop, he'd walked it in heavier boots and with a hand closer to his weapon, but the bones of the place were the same.

Tonight, though…

Tonight, every shadow felt like it was listening.

Not hostile.

Just aware.

He picked his way along the narrow path, shoulder still aching, ribs tender from the last crossing. Pine branches brushed his jacket, whispering against the fabric. Somewhere off to his right, an owl called once, then went silent.

Jay stopped.

There. On the ridge line.

A sound that did not belong to his time.

Hooooom.

Low. Mournful. Stretching out across the treetops like a wind that carried memory with it.

The horn.

Not from the past.

Here.

Now.

Jay's breath caught.

He turned slowly toward the sound, scanning the black line of trees that marked the edge of the higher ground. Nothing moved. No lantern light. No silhouette.

Just that echo, still vibrating in his chest.

He should have been terrified.

Part of him was.

But another part—one shaped by his Christian upbringing and old Salish teachings both—responded not with fear, but with recognition.

His mother's Bible had taught him to pray without ceasing.

His grandfather's stories had taught him to listen without speaking.

He did both.

He bowed his head slightly, the way his mom had when sitting in the pews of a tiny white church off-reservation.

"Lord," he whispered, "if this is something I'm supposed to face… don't let me screw it up."

Then he lifted his gaze to the dark ridge and spoke in halting Salish, the words rusty but sincere.

"Who walks there?" he called softly.

"What do you seek?"

The forest swallowed his voice.

The echoes died quickly, as though the trees themselves did not want to repeat his question.

The horn did not answer again.

But the silence that followed had weight—like standing in a hallway where someone you couldn't see was holding their breath, deciding whether to step closer or turn away.

Jay stood there a while longer, just listening.

No response came.

After a time, he turned and continued toward home…

But the hairs on the back of his neck stayed standing until he stepped out of the tree line and onto the gravel of his driveway.

Something had heard him.

And it wasn't done.

Chapter 15 A Warning From The Old Man

By morning, Jay had convinced himself half of what he'd felt in the trees was exhaustion, adrenaline, and too many nights of jumping between centuries.

The other half—the part that trusted his gut more than the clock—wasn't letting it go.

He drove out to the small cluster of homes where many of the elders lived, the old Agency housing that had been patched, repainted, and re-patched so many times it looked like a quilt in wood and siding.

Old Man Michael's place sat at the far edge, nearest the woods. A crooked split-rail fence half-heartedly kept the deer away from the small garden out back. Smoke drifted from the metal chimney pipe, straight and steady into the cold morning air.

Jay parked and walked around to the rear.

Michael sat in his usual spot—on an overturned milk crate beside a shallow fire pit, feeding cedar chips into the flames with a slow, steady rhythm. He wore an old Army jacket over a plaid shirt, braids tied back with rawhide.

He didn't look up when Jay approached.

"You walk heavy today," Michael said instead. "Like a man carrying two days at once."

"Something like that," Jay said, easing himself down onto a nearby stump. His ribs pulled as he sat. He hid the wince.

Michael tossed another chip into the fire.

"Well?" he asked. "You going to talk, or you just need to borrow my silence for a while?"

Jay took a breath.

He told him.

Not everything—he still hadn't found a way to explain the full extent of the river's pull to anyone but Elder Mary-Two-Rivers—but enough.

He spoke of the horn on the ridge, the echo in the trees, the disturbed graves down by the river, the way the air had shifted when he'd felt that shadow in the timber in the other time.

Michael listened without interrupting, dark eyes fixed on the fire.

When Jay finished, the old man sat quiet for a long moment.

Then he nodded, once.

"You met one of the wanderers," Michael said.

"The wanderers?" Jay echoed.

"Old men," Michael said. "Old women, too, sometimes. They walk the ridges when something has been stirred that should have stayed asleep. Sometimes people see them. Sometimes only the dogs do."

Jay thought of the village, of the shadow, of the horn that had cut the spirit loose from the boy.

"The horn isn't just for messages, is it?" Jay asked.

Michael's gaze slid sideways to him, studying.

"Who told you that?" he asked.

"I heard it," Jay said. "In the trees. Here. And… elsewhere."

Michael grunted, as if that confirmed something he'd already suspected.

"That horn can call the living to council," he said. "But it can also call the dead back where they belong… if they've been disturbed."

A memory flashed in Jay's mind—the broken stones around the modern grave scar, the bones half-exposed to the sky.

"Someone dug up part of the old burial ground by the river," Jay said. "Did you know that?"

Michael's face darkened.

"I feared it," he murmured. "Didn't want to be right."

"Who would do that?" Jay pressed.

"People who think old bones are stories they can own," Michael said bitterly. "Collectors. Researchers. Sometimes our own children, when they chase money more than respect." He shook his head. "Graves are for resting. Not for digging."

"The wanderer said something was bound there," Jay recalled. "Something older than us, older than them. Not evil. Just… dangerous. A spirit without memory, wandering between worlds."

Michael's hand tightened on the cedar chip.

"That's what happens when you pull something from where it belongs and don't put it back right," he said. "Sometimes the dead get lost. Sometimes… something else rides along with them."

Jay let that sink in.

"If it attaches to someone," he said slowly, repeating what the wanderer had warned in the other world, "it feeds on sorrow. Guilt. Wounds that never healed."

Michael nodded.

"Broken things like broken things," he said simply. "They understand each other."

Jay thought of the boy in the village—eyes distant, soul half-absent. Thought of the families here in 1984, generations deep in grief and resentment, some of it earned, some of it inherited.

"Why me?" he asked before he could stop himself. "Why do the wanderers show themselves to me?"

Michael studied him for a long time.

"You walk with one foot in church and one foot in the old ways," the elder said finally. "You wear a badge for the government, but your blood remembers something older. Men like that… sometimes the world uses them as bridges."

Jay snorted softly. "Feels more like a chew toy than a bridge, some days."

Michael's lips twitched in the ghost of a smile.

"You prayed last night," he said.

Jay blinked. "You weren't there."

"Didn't have to be," Michael said. "I can see it on you. People wear their prayers. They hang off them like smoke."

Jay looked at the fire, thinking of his whispered plea in the trees, to a God with nail scars and to whatever else was listening in the dark.

"So what do I do now?" he asked quietly. "You're the one who's seen more winters than anyone. You tell me: how do I fix this?"

Michael leaned forward, resting his elbows on his knees.

"You don't fix it," he said. "You help put it back where it belongs. That's different." He pointed a finger at Jay's chest. "And you don't do it alone."

"I don't exactly have a spirit removal squad on payroll," Jay muttered.

"You have elders," Michael said. "You have people who still remember how to sing the old songs. And you have your own ways of praying. All of that together? That's how you guide it back." He paused. "But first…"

"First what?" Jay asked.

Michael dropped the cedar into the flames.

"You find out who disturbed the grave," he said, voice low and hard. "Because until you know who called it… you won't know where it's going next."

Jay watched the smoke curl upward. In it, he thought he saw shapes—horns, shadows, tears. Probably imagination. Or maybe the smoke was telling truths again, just like Birch-Woman had said.

Either way, he knew one thing:

The wanderer, the horn, the grave, the shadow, the boy, the disturbed burial site in his time—

They were all threads of the same rope.

And he was already holding on.

Chapter 16 The Missionary's Daughter

Traffic on the road into the tribal agency had been light that afternoon. A stillness that either meant the last of the locals had gone home for the day or someone was up to something and no one wanted to talk about it yet.

Jay pulled into the gravel lot, dust kicking up in the rear of his patrol unit. It smelled like late autumn—burnt grass, wet cedar, early snow coming down from the mountains.

He climbed out of the car.

Behind him, a truck pulled into the lot. White Chevy pickup, older model Jay hadn't seen around for years.

His breath caught.

Sarah McAllister stepped out of the driver's side door.

Older, maybe twenty-four, twenty-five. Hair tied back in a loose braid, worn leather jacket and jeans. Dark around the eyes and not sleeping well, worn around the edges like someone who'd been living half a life for too long.

"Sarah?" Jay called.

She turned, eyes wide and startled. Relief so sharp it nearly buckled her knees.

"Jay… thank God."

She walked toward him quickly, clutching a worn leather satchel to her chest like it contained the last piece of her sanity.

Jay hadn't seen her since she was seventeen, when the family had been transferred to another mission post. Had always thought she was different from the rest, more thoughtful, more willing to listen than lecture, more inclined to ask than tell.

But… now.

Now she looked like she'd seen something she wasn't ready for.

"What's wrong?" Jay asked softly.

She drew in a shaky breath.

"My father," she said. "I… found something. Something he wrote. Before he died. And I—don't know what to do with it."

She pulled the satchel out with trembling hands and untied the leather thong.

"He kept it hidden," she whispered. "Even from my mother."

Jay steered her into the agency building and into the back office. Shut the door quietly behind them.

"Sit," he said.

She sat.

Jay placed the papers on the desk. They looked delicate, like anything more than a whisper would destroy them.

He undid the thong.

Pages. Yellowed with age, and tied with string.

Journal pages. Handwritten by Reverend McAllister.

Some were simple, mundane observations about tribal life.

Others were… personal. More hesitant.

Then, toward the end…

Different.

Panic. Confusion. The words of a man possessed by something that was too real to deny, too impossible to believe.

Jay read:

"There is a spirit here the elders do not speak of."

"Something tied to the bones beneath the ridge."

"They say the horn is blown only when it returns."

"God help me, I heard it tonight."

Sarah hugged herself more tightly.

"My father… wasn't a superstitious man," she said softly. "He believed in angels and demons, of course. But this was different. He came to believe whatever he heard wasn't from his Bible at all."

Jay flipped to the last page of the journal.

The final entry had been so haphazardly scrawled the pen had ripped the paper.

"If they sound the horn again, it means the same spirit has returned."

"The one from the old grave."

"The one that hungers for sorrow."

Jay sucked in a breath.

The horn.

The grave.

The shadow that hungered for sorrow.

Sarah leaned forward, voice quavering.

"Jay, I heard it last night."

His heart hammered.

"Horn or shadow?" Jay asked quietly.

She swallowed. "Both."

The room seemed to close in around them.

Jay rubbed his jaw, thinking fast.

"Where?" he asked.

"The ridge behind my parents' old house," she whispered. "I went out to see. The ground was disturbed. Someone had been digging."

Jay felt the earth drop from under him.

The same ridge he'd seen from the helicopter.

The same grave Birch-Woman had warned him of.

The same spirit the wanderer had been trying to hold at bay.

Two worlds.

One wound.

Sarah looked up at him suddenly, eyes shining.

"My father wasn't crazy, was he?"

Jay closed the journal.

"No," he said. "He was right."

Which seemed to bring her both relief… and terror.

Chapter 17 The Disturbance

They drove.

Jay following behind her in his patrol unit while she led the way in her old Chevy. He didn't want to leave her alone if anything went down—but also he needed to be able to shine a light on whatever was in front of them.

The ridge was less than a mile from the agency— close enough Jay wondered how many people walked past every day without knowing what lay beneath their feet.

Sarah pulled over near the trailhead. Jay parked behind her.

She climbed out of the truck slowly, almost hesitantly, as if the very earth might be judging her steps.

"This way," she said.

They followed the overgrown path toward the ridge. Jay held his flashlight, though twilight still hung in the trees blue.

Silence fell with every step. No birds. No insects. Even the wind held its breath.

At last Sarah stopped at a small clearing.

"This is it," she whispered.

Jay stepped forward.

The ground was disturbed.

Fresh dirt.

Roots torn up.

In the center of the disturbance—

A long rectangular cut into the earth.

A grave.

Freshly dug.

Freshly unearthed.

Jay crouched, shining his light on the soil.

Something pale peeked from the ground.

Bone.

Not clean bone—old bone. Worn. Ancient.

Sarah knelt down beside him, swallowing hard.

"This is the place," she said. "The one my father wrote about."

Jay reached out to touch the exposed bone—

—and pulled his hand back with a start as a cold pulse shot into his fingertips.

Sarah gasped. "What was that?"

Jay flexed out his hand, heart still pounding.

"Not natural," he said. "It's attached to something. It's… awake."

Sarah took a step back.

"What do we do?"

Jay stood up.

He didn't answer at once.

Truth was wrapping around him like a heavy blanket:

The grave disturbed in this world was connected to the grave disturbed in the past.

As if both times were linked to the same knot—and someone had pulled too hard.

Jay swept the flashlight over the rest of the clearing.

More dirt shifted.

Fresh shovel marks.

Someone had been here recently.

Not long ago. Maybe last night.

"Someone's been digging," Jay murmured. "Not long ago. Maybe last night."

Sarah paused. Then asked the question Jay didn't want to consider.

"Do you think… whoever dug it up… called that spirit back?"

He didn't mince words.

"Yes."

"And now it's loose?" she whispered.

He nodded.

"And it's looking for something. Or someone."

She hugged herself.

"Jay… the shadow I heard…" She glanced toward the trees. "It wasn't just watching. It was following me."

Jay's stomach twisted.

"Did it touch you?" he asked sharply.

"No," she said. "But it… reached toward me. Like it knew my name."

Something stirred in the trees.

Jay tensed.

Sarah froze.

Jay raised the flashlight, sweeping it across the timber.

Nothing.

But the air had shifted, cold, dense, heavy with something unseen but all too present.

"Stay behind me," Jay said quietly.

Sarah stepped toward him.

A shadow flickered in the pines.

Jay raised his hand. "There."

Another flicker.

Closer.

The boy had been targeted because he was open, new, full of unguarded sorrow.

Sarah…

She carried sorrow too.

Her father's death.

Her confusion.

Her fear.

She was vulnerable.

"Jay…" she whispered. "I feel it."

He put his hand on her arm.

"Don't look at it," he said.

But she did.

A figure stood between the trees.

Just within the shadows.

Not a man.

Not quite a spirit.

Something like absence taking shape—shifting, flickering, incomplete.

Sarah gasped.

Jay grabbed her wrist.

"Back up," he said.

"I can't," she whispered. "It's—Jay, it's calling to me."

The figure stepped half into the light.

Jay could see its form clearly now.

Faceless.

Just darkness shaped like sorrow.

"Sarah—look at me," Jay ordered.

She refused to move.

The shadow tilted its head, studying her.

And Jay understood in that moment—

It wasn't here for Sarah.

It was here for him.

His sorrow.

His guilt.

His failures.

The weight he'd been carrying in both worlds.

"Come on, then," Jay growled at it. "Take your best shot."

The shadow twitched at his voice—

Then the horn sounded.

Deep.

Ancient.

Nearby.

Sarah staggered as if the sound had struck her physically.

Jay held her steady, gaze never leaving the spirit.

The horn called again.

The shadow twitched—

Then dissolved into a dark swirl that shot back into the trees.

Gone.

Sarah clung to Jay's jacket, breathing hard.

He held her for a moment, just until her shaking subsided.

At last she whispered:

"That wasn't the same horn I heard last night."

Jay stared into the pines.

"No," he said quietly. "That one was on our side."

Sarah swallowed. "Then the other horn…?"

Jay nodded grimly.

"The other horn is calling the shadow."

She shuddered. "Who's blowing it?"

Jay didn't reply.

Because he didn't know yet.

But he would.

He had to.

For the boy.

For Weyan.

For Sarah.

For both worlds.

And for whoever had woken something that should have stayed buried.

Chapter 18 Return Of The Wanderer

The night was thin.

It felt like the world had been pulled taut over something shifting underneath.

Jay had left Sarah at her parents' old house with very clear instructions:

"Lights on. Doors locked. If you hear the horn again, call me or Michael. Stay inside. Don't go outside by yourself. Not for anything."

She'd nodded, fingers still white-knuckled on the strap of her satchel.

"Jay," she'd said quietly, "if my father knew this was real… do you think he was afraid?"

"Yes," Jay had said honestly. "And I think he tried to protect people anyway."

She'd looked at him for a long moment, then whispered:

"Just… don't let it get me."

"I won't," he'd said.

He hoped he was telling the truth.

Now he walked alone beneath the trees behind his own small house, drawn by the faint pull he'd learned to recognize — the same tug that brought him to the river, the same sense that something was waiting.

The moon slipped through the clouds in ragged patches, illuminating the forest in shards of silver and shadow. Needles muffled his steps, softening his approach.

He didn't call out.

Some meetings didn't need an invitation.

The horn sounded once.

Not loud — but close.

Jay stopped.

The wanderer emerged from between two thick pines.

As if he'd just walked in from another century and found the trail still warm.

He wore the same furs, the same weathered leather, the same antler-horn strapped across his chest. His hair was threaded with gray feathers. His face was a collage of lines carved by time and weather, but his eyes were clear and sharp.

He looked exactly as he did in the past.

Jay exhaled slowly.

"Figured it was you," he said.

The wanderer studied him for a long, quiet moment.

"You have been busy," he said in accented English, his voice rough but steady. "Too busy for one man."

"Story of my life," Jay answered. "You're walking both sides now, huh?"

The wanderer's gaze slid over the trees, the distant glow of the town, the faint power line humming like a nervous snake across the ridge.

"Your world is loud," he said. "Even when it is quiet."

Jay huffed a humorless laugh. "Yeah. That's about right."

The wanderer's attention returned to him.

"They woke it," he said.

Jay's chest tightened.

"Not the ancestors," the wanderer added. "Something older."

"Your spirit without a memory," Jay said. "The one bound in the grave."

The wanderer nodded once.

"It was tied between worlds," he said. "Long ago. It did not belong to the living or the dead. So our people bound it where both could watch it."

"Until someone dug it up," Jay muttered.

"Yes."

They stood in silence as the wind rustled high in the canopy.

"Is that why it keeps going after the boy?" Jay asked. "Why it followed Sarah? Because they're… softer inside?"

The wanderer tilted his head, considering.

"It seeks broken places," he said. "It does not know its own name. It only knows pain. Guilt. Sorrow. It tastes these things… and remembers that it is lost."

Jay thought of the boy in the village, sitting hollow-eyed at the edge of camp.

Thought of Sarah freezing when the shadow slithered near.

Thought of the way his own chest felt like a file cabinet of mistakes.

"And if it attaches itself?" Jay said quietly, repeating what the wanderer had told him in the village.

"It feeds," the wanderer said. "On old wounds. On shame. On the tears that never fell."

"Can it be driven out?" Jay asked.

"Not by steel," the wanderer said. "Not by bullets. Not by your laws." His hand brushed the horn at his chest. "Only by balance. By prayer. By the old ways… and the new."

"Together," Jay said.

"Yes. Together."

The wanderer stepped closer, studying Jay's face as if searching for something.

"You walk two worlds," he said. "Two fires in one body. Two ways of praying in one heart. Spirit listening… and church words." He nodded. "The river chose you for this."

Jay shifted, suddenly uncomfortable under the weight of that.

"I never asked for any of this," he muttered.

"No one ever does," the wanderer replied. "But someone always must carry it."

The wind sighed through the trees.

"So how do we do it?" Jay asked. "How do we get this thing off the boy… away from Sarah… back where it belongs?"

The wanderer's eyes darkened.

"We call it," he said. "Where we can hold it."

"That sounds… awful," Jay said.

"It will be dangerous," the wanderer agreed. "But the spirit is already hunting. Better to meet it on ground we choose."

Jay exhaled slowly.

"Where?" he asked.

The wanderer looked toward the river.

And beyond it.

"Inside the steam," he said. "In the heart of the lodge. Fire. Stone. Water. Word."

"A sweat," Jay said.

"Yes. But not one world alone." The wanderer's gaze sharpened. "Your people have your own way of reaching. Your own… words." His hand gestured upward. "Your own cross. Your own songs. Bring them. Stand with us in both ways."

Jay swallowed.

He hadn't been in a sweat in years.

Hadn't heard a hymn in just as long.

And now he was being asked to stand in the center of both.

"And if I say no?" he asked quietly.

The wanderer glanced at the trees.

"Then it will find its own path," he said. "Through the boy. Through the woman. Through you." His voice hardened. "And it will not stop until it forgets what it was chasing."

Jay pictured the village burning in the past.

Pictured Sarah's hollow eyes in the present.

Pictured the boy staring into the trees, listening to horns no one else could hear.

"I'll be there," he said.

The wanderer's shoulders dropped a fraction, as if a small weight had eased.

"Two lodges," he said. "Two times. Same spirit. We begin when the night is deepest. When the veil is thin."

Jay nodded.

"I'll bring who I can," he said. "Elders. People who still remember the old songs. Maybe… one or two who know the Jesus ones, too."

The wanderer's mouth twitched in the ghost of a wry smile.

"Then perhaps," he said, "we will confuse it enough to send it home."

He stepped back into the shadows.

"Walk careful until then, River-Warden," he said. "It will feel you gathering."

"You see it if it comes near me?" Jay asked.

The wanderer tapped the horn.

"I will hear," he said.

Then he stepped backward into the dark, and in three breaths, was gone.

The trees shivered.

As Jay turned toward home, he knew sleep was a lost cause.

He wasn't just a cop anymore.

He wasn't just a man lost between centuries.

He was about to stand in the middle of a circle meant for something that had no name.

And try to send it back.

Chapter 19 Into The Steam

They gathered on both sides of time.

In the past, the lodge by the river glowed faintly, a round shadow against the deeper night. Willow ribs bent and crossed, draped in hides, sealed tight. Outside, firelight licked at the darkness, heating the pile of rounded river stones until they burned orange at the core.

Weyan stood by the entrance, lips moving in a quiet song as she laid cedar boughs along the ground. Talek carried water in a carved wooden bowl. Birch-Woman traced symbols in the dirt that Jay didn't fully understand but felt with every nerve.

In the present, another lodge had been built—not far from where the old grave lay.

Old Man Michael had commanded that part.

"We'll do it right," he'd said. "No shortcuts. If we're going to call something like that into the steam, everything has to be in order."

Sarah helped carry stones, face pale but jaw set. A few younger men stood by, watching nervously. Elder Mary-Two-Rivers had come as well, wrapped in a worn wool shawl, eyes calm and fierce at the same time.

Jay moved between them in both worlds, like a needle stitching across fabric.

He could feel the echo—one lodge layered over the other, separated by centuries, connected by intention.

Same river.

Same ridge.

Same grave.

"We begin when the horn sounds," Michael said.

"In my time too," the wanderer told Jay on the other side.

"Remember," Elder Mary-Two-Rivers added in the present, "you don't fight it with anger. You guide it with balance."

"And prayer," Michael said.

"Both kinds," she agreed, glancing at Jay with a small smile.

His heart pounded.

He had prayed in the back of patrol cars, in ER waiting rooms, in the silence after bad news.

He had listened to elders pray over fires, over sick children, over the land itself.

Never like this.

Never with the possibility that something without a face might answer.

Night deepened.

Stars peered out between torn clouds.

The wanderer appeared near the lodge in the past, horn at his chest.

Michael moved beside the modern one, cedar in hand.

The air grew heavy.

The boy sat near the entrance of the past lodge, flanked by Weyan and Talek, both of whom had made it clear with spear and knife and body language that nothing would touch him without going through them first.

Sarah sat just inside the present lodge, near Mary-Two-Rivers, fingers wrapped so tight around the small cross at her neck her knuckles had gone white.

Jay knelt at the doorway of both lodges, feeling his heartbeat sync up in a way it had never done before.

Between worlds, the river hummed.

"Now," the wanderer said.

Michael nodded without hearing the word, but knowing all the same.

The horn blew.

Deep.

Low.

A note that seemed to pass through dirt and bone, water and memory.

Inside the lodges, the heated stones were carried in— glowing, hissing as they met the damp earth.

The doors closed.

Darkness.

Then—

Water dropped onto stone.

Steam exploded upward, hot and wet, filling the small enclosed spaces with breath and heat and the smell of earth and cedar and sweat.

In both times, songs began.

In the past, Weyan and Birch-Woman sang an old, rolling melody that seemed to wrap around Jay like a woven blanket. In the present, Michael and Mary-Two-Rivers began a low chant, words in Salish, words of grounding and asking, words that felt like home and warning at once.

Jay knelt, sweat already beading on his forehead.

He bowed his head.

And he prayed.

"Jesus," he whispered, "Son of God, who sees things I can't… be here. Not just for me. For them. For the boy. For Sarah. Don't let this thing take what isn't its."

Then, without a pause, he shifted into the old language, the one his grandfather had pressed into his ears as a child.

He prayed for balance.

For guidance.

For the spirit that was lost to find its road instead of tearing through everyone else's.

Outside, the horn sounded again.

The steam shifted.

The temperature dropped so suddenly the hairs on Jay's arms leapt up.

It was here.

He didn't see it at first.

He felt it.

A pressure at the edge of the circle.

Then at the center of his chest.

A weight pressing down, trying to pry him open from the inside.

In the past, the boy gasped, clutching his heart. Weyan wrapped an arm around him, her song never faltering.

In the present, Sarah stiffened, eyes flying open in the dark.

"Jay," she whispered. "I feel it."

"So do I," he gritted.

The shadow took shape in the steam.

Not as a man.

Not as a monster.

As a wound.

A jagged, black tear in the air that seemed to pulse with trapped sobs and swallowed screams.

It pressed against Jay, searching.

Old guilt rose fast.

Things he'd done and left undone. Calls he hadn't made in time. Faces of people he'd found too late, bodies already gone. Words he wished he'd spoken. Apologies he never had the courage to give.

He saw the mother whose son he couldn't save.

The elder he hadn't believed in time.

A boy in another century looking at him with trust so naked it was almost painful.

The spirit latched onto all of it, drinking it in like water.

Jay's hands dug into the dirt.

"No," he ground out.

He forced his thoughts away from himself.

Not my sorrow. Not mine.

He focused on the boy in the past, on the child's laughter before the shadow ever noticed him. Focused on Sarah's stubborn compassion. On Weyan's courage. On Talek's evolving trust. On Michael's steady presence. On Mary-Two-Rivers' patient, fierce belief.

He filled his mind with them instead of his own failings.

"You don't belong in us," he told the spirit. "You belong on your own road."

In the past, the wanderer blew the horn again, this time in a short, sharp burst.

In the present, Michael lifted his own voice louder, chanting words that spoke of return, of setting things right, of bones resting where they should.

Mary-Two-Rivers laid a hand on Sarah's shoulder. "Don't cling to it," she whispered. "Let it pass through. Let it go."

The shadow shuddered.

It turned from Jay, reaching instinctively for the richer, easier veins of human pain around it.

The boy spasmed once, then gasped as if coming up from drowning.

Sarah sobbed, once, a single choked sound—then inhaled a long, shuddery breath and went still.

"Come on," Jay whispered. "Come on, you don't have to stay stuck like this. You're not them. You're not us. You're something else. Go where you belong."

He didn't know if spirits listened to reason.

But something in it shifted.

Under the songs and horn and layered prayers, something in the wound woke to the idea that it was, in fact, separate. That it did not have to live only by feeding from others.

The steam swirled.

The tear in the air loosened.

Jay felt it pull away from his chest, felt it uncurl from around the boy's heart, felt it lift its weight from Sarah's lungs.

Then—

Up.

Through the darkness of the lodge.

Into the narrow cracks between cedar branches and hides.

Out.

In the past, the spirit erupted into the night like a dark breath. The stars seemed to dim briefly, then brightened again as if relieved.

In the present, the steam above their heads thinned, carrying something with it—a heaviness leaving the circle.

Outside, the horn sounded one last time.

A low, descending note.

Not a call.

A farewell.

Inside the lodge, the air slowly warmed again.

Silence settled between songs.

Someone exhaled—a long, low release no one had realized they'd been holding.

The wanderer's voice spoke in the dark of the past lodge.

"It is gone," he said.

Michael's voice echoed, decades later, in the modern one.

"For now," he agreed.

Jay sagged, sweat running down his face like rain. His limbs shook, not just with exhaustion, but with the aftershock of having some invisible thing rifling through the drawers of his soul.

"You okay?" Mary-Two-Rivers asked quietly from the dark.

He managed a rough laugh.

"I've been worse," he said.

In the other time, Weyan reached for his shoulder in the steam.

"You came back," she whispered. "You said you would, and you did."

"Still breathing," he answered.

"And the boy?" she asked.

The child's small voice spoke up, a little hoarse.

"It's quieter in my head," he said. "I can't hear the horn anymore."

"Good," Talek murmured.

In the present, Sarah spoke softly.

"It's… lighter," she said. "Like something let go of my spine."

"Not just yours," Michael said. "It was feeding off more than one of us."

Jay sat up straighter.

"It's gone," he said.

"From here," Mary-Two-Rivers corrected gently. "And from them. That's enough for tonight."

"Enough," Michael echoed.

Outside, the night breathed in again, calm and deep.

The doors of both lodges opened.

Cool air rushed in, carrying with it the smell of pine and river and smoke and a world that, for the moment, had survived another brush with things it wasn't ready to name.

Jay stepped out under the stars—in one time and in the other.

He tilted his head back, feeling the breeze on his face.

"For now," he murmured.

But he knew this wasn't the end.

Someone had disturbed the grave.

Someone had blown the wrong horn.

Someone—a living someone—still held the reason the spirit had come back at all.

Until he found that person…

The river would not be done with him.

And neither would the path between times.

Chapter 20 Tracks In Two Worlds

Dawn — Iron River Ridge

Jay didn't sleep that night.

Not after what had happened in the sweat lodge.

Every time he closed his eyes, he felt that shadow press into his chest again — the weight of old sorrow trying to take root in him. It was gone… for now. But something told him the spirit wasn't finished.

When the first gray light crept over the ridge, he saddled his horse and rode out with Sarah. The wanderer had vanished sometime before sunrise, leaving only the faint impression of moccasin tracks in the dust and the echo of his warning:

"Someone woke it. Someone living."

Jay followed the narrow path through the timber, the ground still damp from night mist. The forest was silent — too silent — as if even the birds were holding their breath.

Sarah rode close, her voice barely above a whisper.

"Do you think the spirit is still out there?"

Jay nodded.

"Spirits don't just disappear. They follow their trail until something sets them right."

Sarah swallowed, gripping the saddle horn tighter.

"My father wrote about things like this… but I thought he exaggerated."

Jay didn't answer.

He didn't need to.

They reached the disturbed burial ground again. The earth still looked wrong. Wounded. The rectangular cut was too clean, too deliberate — someone had dug with tools, not hands.

Jay knelt beside the exposed roots.

Something glinted beneath the fresh dirt.

A fragment of metal.

Modern metal.

Not from the 1800s.

Not from the old days.

He lifted it between his fingers — a piece of a shovel handle, broken and sharp-edged.

Sarah's face paled.

"Jay… that's not tribal. That's from town."

Jay stood slowly, breath turning cold.

"This wasn't grave robbing," he said softly.

"This was searching."

He scanned the ground again — looking for footprints, tire tracks, anything.

Then he saw them.

Boot prints.

Fresh.

Heading deeper into the timber.

But there was something else.

A second set of tracks, overlaying the first.

Wide.

Soft-edged.

Like something had followed the intruder from behind.

Jay crouched low, tracing the impressions with a fingertip.

"The spirit," he murmured. "It followed the one who broke the ground."

Sarah stiffened.

"Is that… bad?"

"Only if it attaches to the wrong person."

Jay didn't realize how hard he was gripping the shovel fragment until his knuckles went white.

He stood abruptly and turned to Sarah.

"We're not tracking just a person," he said. "We're tracking whatever followed them."

The Trail of the Living

They moved deeper into the forest, the light growing warmer but never reaching the ground. The trees leaned close like tall sentinels guarding old secrets.

After an hour, Jay spotted a fresh trail:

• branches snapped at shoulder height

• patches of disturbed moss

• mud smeared on a fallen log

Someone unfamiliar had passed through — someone who didn't know the land and didn't respect its paths.

Sarah whispered, "Who would do this?"

Jay didn't know, but he had guesses:

Grave diggers.

Artifact hunters.

Teenagers messing where they shouldn't.

Or someone looking for a story no one should tell.

Suddenly, Sarah tugged his sleeve.

"Jay… look."

A torn strip of fabric lay caught on a low cedar branch.

Denim.

Dark blue.

From modern jeans.

Jay pocketed it.

Whoever this was… they weren't far.

The First Sign of the Spirit

A few hundred yards farther, the forest temperature changed again — a cold pocket settling around them.

Jay felt it in his bones.

The shadow had passed through here.

He raised a hand to stop Sarah.

"Do you feel that?"

She nodded, hugging herself.

"Like walking into a freezer."

Jay scanned the trees.

And saw it.

Where the boot prints continued forward, the shadow-pattern footprints split off to the right — deeper into the cedar grove.

Two trails now.

Two directions.

Two threats.

Sarah looked at him, eyes wide.

"Which do we follow?"

Jay stared at both paths, heart pounding.

One led to the living.

One led to the restless.

Both could break someone's life if left unchecked.

But then he saw something in the mud beside the boot prints.

A second, smaller footprint — too small to be the intruder.

A child.

Sarah gasped softly.

"Oh no…"

Jay grabbed the reins and swung into the saddle.

"We follow the living first," he said, voice tight.

"Because someone alive just stepped into the middle of all this."

The wind shifted then, carrying something faint but unmistakable:

A boy's cry.

Distant.

Frightened.

Cut short.

Jay's heart slammed against his ribs.

"Ride!" he shouted.

And the two of them tore through the trees —

toward a danger they didn't yet understand,

toward a child who might already be caught,

toward whatever walked the ridge with sorrow as its

skin.

Chapter 21 The Boy In The Cedar Grove

The horses pounded the soft earth, branches slapping against their sides as Jay and Sarah thundered toward the noise. Jay could feel it in the air — that unnatural chill the wanderer had warned them about. It seeped into the ground. Into the air. Into the bones under their feet.

The cedar grove loomed ahead like a wall of dark, living pillars.

Silent.

Watchful.

Jay pulled the horse to a stop.

Sarah slid down from her saddle next to him, breath ragged.

"That scream…" she said. "It sounded like—"

"A boy," Jay finished.

"Hiding. And something behind him."

Jay tied the reins, gestured for silence, and stepped into the cedar grove.

Inside, the world changed.

Air thickened.

Cold dug into their skin.

Sound moved strangely — muffled, distant.

Dark cedar trunks towered in every direction, straight and tall as cathedral pillars. Fallen needles carpeted the ground in a soft, whispering silence beneath their feet.

Jay moved carefully, eyes scanning for tracks.

There — a small footprint.

Another.

The boy had run.

And something had run after him.

Jay gestured for Sarah to stay behind him and followed the trail deeper into the cedar grove. A low hum filled the air, like the sound of someone chanting a prayer too distant to hear clearly.

Sarah's fingers brushed the back of his hand.

"Jay… that sound. It's—"

He raised two fingers.

Stop.

Listen.

The humming grew louder.

Not words.

Not breath.

Not wind.

Something else.

Something hungry.

Jay stepped around a cedar trunk—

And stopped.

The boy crouched in a small clearing, back pressed to the trunk of a massive cedar. He was breathing heavily, hands clenched tight, eyes staring at something in front of him.

Jay followed the boy's gaze—

And saw it.

A shape.

Undefined.

Like smoke trying to remember it had once been something solid.

A shadow with edges that flickered and blurred with the boy's fear.

The spirit.

It hovered just out of reach, swaying with each pulse of cold air. Cedar branches around it creaked, bending inward as though pushed by the same force.

Sarah gasped quietly behind Jay.

The boy whispered, voice shaking:

"Leave me alone... I didn't take anything... I didn't..."

Jay stepped into the clearing.

"Hey," he said softly. "You're alright. I'm here."

The boy jerked toward the sound of his voice — and the shadow with him, as if sensing the change.

Jay raised both hands slowly.

"It can't hurt you if you don't feed it," he said, voice calm, steady, the same tone he'd used dozens of times in his police years. "Don't give it your fear."

The boy shook his head violently.

"I didn't do anything!"

Jay took another step.

"I know. Someone else disturbed the ground. Someone else woke it."

The shadow twisted, moving closer.

Sarah whispered, "Jay…"

Jay kept his voice low.

"What's your name?" he asked the boy.

The boy hesitated, terrified — then whispered:

"David."

Jay nodded.

"David, I need you to look at me. Not it. Me."

The boy tore his gaze from the shadow and focused on Jay. Slowly. Painfully.

The spirit recoiled — just an inch — as if the shift in attention weakened it.

Jay stepped closer.

"That's it," he said. "You're not alone out here."

But the shadow surged suddenly, a cold wave rolling through the cedar grove. The cedar needles trembled. Sarah staggered back, clutching her arms.

Jay felt it too — a pressure pushing against his mind, trying to dig into wounds he'd buried long ago.

You've failed before.

You couldn't save them.

You can't save him.

Jay clenched his jaw.

"Not today," he growled.

He stepped between the boy and the spirit.

"David," he said, voice firm, "go to Sarah. Go now."

Sarah reached her hand out.

The boy bolted toward her, stumbling into her arms.

The shadow shrieked without sound — a violent, trembling distortion in the air — and shot forward toward Jay.

Jay didn't move.

Instead, he breathed once, deeply, and spoke the Salish prayer he had learned beside the elder:

"tšəɫət sťáx̣ʷ — go back to your path.

This is not your place.

Not your time."

The shadow quivered.

Jay felt the cold rush through him, searching for weakness — guilt, sorrow, old wounds — but the prayer held strong.

The cedar trees creaked again, louder, like old doors settling.

Sarah whispered sharply:

"Jay—look!"

The spirit faltered.

And then—

It withdrew.

Fading like smoke, drawn backward into the darker part of the cedar grove, slipping between cedar trunks until it vanished entirely.

Jay exhaled hard, knees nearly buckling.

Sarah held David close, both of them trembling.

Jay walked to them and knelt so he was eye level with the boy.

"You did nothing wrong," he said softly. "Someone else woke it. Someone who shouldn't have been digging where they had no right."

David nodded shakily, tears streaking his face.

Behind them, the cedar grove grew quiet again — but not calm.

Not safe.

Just… waiting.

Jay stood slowly, scanning the fading tracks left by the spirit.

"It's not done," he said quietly.

Sarah swallowed.

"What now?"

Jay tightened his jaw, eyes fixed on the direction the shadow had fled.

"Now," he said, "we find whoever disturbed that grave."

He looked back toward the boy.

"And we make sure it never touches another child."

Chapter 22 The Bootprint In The Mud

Cedar Grove — Morning Light

For a long moment, none of them moved.

The cedar grove had gone still, like the forest was holding its breath after the shadow fled. Jay finally exhaled and touched the boy's shoulder, reassuring him with a quiet nod.

"You're safe now," he said.

But in his chest, the warning remained:

This wasn't finished. Not even close.

Sarah held the boy's trembling hand, helping him steady his steps. "We should get him back to the village," she whispered.

Jay shook his head.

"Not yet. Something brought him out here. I need to know who else was in these woods."

He turned sharply, scanning the ground. Beneath the cedar needles, the prints were faint, but they were there — a pattern that didn't belong.

Deep heel.

Thick tread.

Square edges.

A modern boot.

Sarah stepped beside him. "Jay… that's not from the old days. That's someone from now."

Jay nodded slowly.

"Someone who shouldn't be out here."

He crouched, brushing his fingers over the damp mud. The print was fresh — maybe a day old at most — pressed deep from weight and haste. A trail of indentations stretched north through the trees.

But what bothered him wasn't just the bootprint.

It was what sat inside it.

A thin layer of cold frost.

Frost that shouldn't exist in daylight.

Sarah saw it too.

"Oh God," she whispered. "Jay… the spirit was following him."

The wandering shadow had taken interest in this trail.

And shadows from the old world didn't attach to just anyone.

Jay's voice turned steady, hardened by duty.

"Let's move."

He ushered the boy ahead of Sarah and began following the track.

The Trail Grows Strange

The bootprints cut through the cedar grove, weaving between the trees like the intruder had been running — or being chased. The disturbed earth was erratic, patches of torn moss, broken limbs hanging low.

Sarah looked around nervously.

"You think he knew he woke something?"

"No," Jay said. "People who dig into old graves never think about the consequences. They only think about what they can take."

"And the spirit… it followed him because of that?"

Jay didn't answer — but the look in his eyes said yes.

After a hundred yards, the prints crossed a shallow, slow-moving creek. Jay paused at the bank.

The water rippled with no breeze.

A small swirl moved in the center, as if stirred by something unseen.

Sarah's voice trembled.

"Is it still here?"

Jay crouched and dipped two fingers into the water.

Ice shot through his hand.

He pulled back sharply.

"It was here," he said. "Recent. Minutes ago… maybe less."

David, still catching his breath, tucked himself close behind Sarah.

Jay pointed downstream.

"The intruder went that way."

But something caught Sarah's eye.

"Jay… look."

Across the creek, a second set of tracks emerged — not bootprints. Not footprints at all.

Shallow impressions like weightless feet dragging through the soil.

Jay's pulse tightened.

The spirit had crossed the water, following the intruder's path.

"Two trails," Sarah whispered. "Just like before."

Jay nodded.

"One leads to a person. One leads to trouble."

He stepped across the creek.

"We're following both."

A Clue in the Alder Trees

The trail led into a thicket of alder trees, their trunks pale and thin in the morning glow. The boots had trampled through the brush without care, snapping branches and leaving a clear, reckless path.

Jay spotted something half-buried under fallen leaves.

A torn piece of denim.

Same material as the scrap caught on the cedar branch earlier.

He lifted it.

Sarah leaned in. "It matches the fabric from the burial site."

"Same person," Jay said. "Whoever dug that grave, this is their trail."

But the spirit trail was harder to read — just faint marks in the earth, subtle disturbances in the moss, slight indentations where cold air had settled.

The two trails remained close — too close.

Sarah whispered, "It's tracking him. Like a hunter."

Jay nodded.

"Spirits attach to emotion. Fear. Guilt. Pain. If he's carrying any of that — and most grave robbers do — it'll stay on him until something breaks the bond."

David swallowed, still shaking.

"Is… is it gonna hurt him?"

Jay stood, looking deeper into the timber.

"That depends on what he does next."

The First Human Sign

A stray glint in the brush caught Jay's eye.

He pushed aside a branch and found something lodged in the moss:

A flashlight.

New.

Mud-splattered.

Still warm from use.

Sarah frowned.

"That's… definitely from today."

Jay clicked the switch.

Nothing.

Dead battery.

But the mud on the casing was still damp — meaning the intruder had dropped it less than an hour ago.

Jay scanned the ground again — and saw a new bootprint.

Deep.

Hurried.

Heading uphill toward the ridge.

Sarah's breath hitched.

"He's close."

Jay nodded slowly.

"And scared."

David tugged on Sarah's sleeve. "Ms. Sarah… is he bad?"

Sarah hesitated — and Jay answered for her.

"People do bad things for different reasons. But whatever he took, whatever he woke… we need to stop him before he does something worse."

Jay stepped forward again, boots crunching through alder leaves.

And then —

a long, mournful sound drifted through the trees.

Not the spirit.

Not the wind.

A horn.

Jay froze.

Sarah's eyes went wide.

"The wanderer?" she whispered.

Jay listened.

Three notes.

Slow.

Heavy.

A warning.

Jay tightened his grip on the flashlight.

"No," he said, voice low. "That wasn't for us."

He stared up the ridge where the bootprints led.

"That was meant for the one we're following."

Sarah shivered.

"Why would he warn him?"

Jay's jaw tightened, dread seeping down his spine.

"Because whatever woke up might already be with him."

He looked at David — frightened, trusting, clinging to Sarah's hand.

Then he looked back to the trail.

"Let's move," he said.

"Before the spirit finds him first."

And the three of them climbed the ridge toward a danger neither world had prepared them for.

Chapter 23 The Ridge Of Echoes

Why this one works best right now:

Jay is on the trail of the living intruder, and now it's time to find out what he was after.

The spirit's presence is intensifying — but we don't need the wanderer again for a while.

Let the tension build.

The ridge has a history… and the digging wasn't random.

This chapter gives you the opportunity to drop the first big clue to a larger mystery, possibly tied to Jay's tribe, or Sarah's missionary father, or even the river itself.

This chapter is designed to set the reader up for Chapter 25 to bring back the wanderer with a vengeance.

Let's do this.

Chapter 24 The Ridge Of Echoes

Upper Ridge — Late Morning

The ascent had become more gradual as Jay followed the boot trail up the ridge. David hung back to stay close to Sarah, one hand in her coat and the other clutching a cedar twig the wanderer had once described as a shield for fearful hearts.

The farther they climbed, the more unfamiliar the forest became.

No birds.

No insects.

No wind.

Only the lightest rustle of something unseen moving just beyond the treeline, a shadow present and yet not present.

Jay slowed as the trail thinned out on a shelf of rock.

"Careful step," he cautioned. "The prints are fresher back here."

Sarah's eyes darted across the moss. "And colder."

She was right.

The frost around the bootprints was thicker — a faint white halo that had to be the early breath of winter settling on the ground.

Jay crouched to the edge of a print, letting his fingertips graze the soil.

A chill coursed into his fingers.

"He was running," Jay said. "Hard. Something frightened him."

Sarah swallowed. "The spirit?"

"Or something else."

David's small voice quivered. "I heard him… earlier. I think he cried."

Jay's stomach tightened.

He didn't want the boy involved in this any longer — but the boy had been part of the threat before Jay even knew there was a threat to track.

Jay rose slowly to his feet.

"We keep moving. But you stay back by me."

As they reached the top of the final rise, the ridge split open into a clearing, an area where the trees shrank away from the center, as though carved centuries ago by something no wind could touch.

Jay stopped.

The ground was a scar.

More disturbed earth.

More shovel marks.

A large circle of soil, upturned then clumsily replaced.

But this time — not a grave.

A cache pit.

An old one.

Jay's chest tightened with an old, familiar dread.

"Someone was looking for something," he whispered.

Sarah crouched beside the hole, brushing the soil aside with care.

"Jay… this wasn't a burial site. My father wrote about these."

Jay nodded slowly.

"Elder caches. Hidden supplies. Medicine bundles. Warrior belongings."

Sarah rubbed her fingers over a carved piece of old wood jutting out from the edge of the pit. Symbols had been scraped into it — Salish markings, faint but still vibrant with significance.

"Jay," she whispered, "this belonged to your people."

Jay knelt beside her, taking a deep breath.

He brushed away more soil until the full carving emerged — an old cedar lid, cracked but whole.

He could feel the worn groove of it beneath his thumb.

"We don't dig these up," Jay said. "Ever. Not unless it's the one who buried it… or someone chosen by them."

He lifted the lid, slow as a man unwrapping a history both ancient and sacred.

The inside was only dirt and cedar fibers.

Empty.

Sarah sucked in a breath.

"He already took what was here."

Jay rose slowly to his feet, every muscle in his body coiling.

A human had taken something sacred.

Something hidden for generations.

Something strong enough to draw a spirit out of rest.

He scanned the clearing again — searching for what the intruder had been after.

Then he spotted it.

A second set of markings.

Faint.

Scratched into a stone near the pit.

Jay stepped closer, squinting.

Not tribal.

Not spiritual.

Letters.

English letters.

"M.M."

Sarah's breath caught in her throat.

"Those… those are my father's initials."

Jay froze.

M.M.

McAllister.

The missionary.

The man who took notes about wanderers.

The man who had warned Sarah that spirits return when old ground is broken.

Jay stared at the stone.

"Your father was here," he said.

"Years ago… or maybe he left this as a warning."

Sarah dropped to her knees beside him, her voice shaking.

"If he knew this place was dangerous… why didn't he warn the tribe?"

Jay's jaw clenched.

"That's not the question."

He pointed to the fresh bootprints leading away from the pit.

"The question is: who would go back to his notes?"

David tugged on Sarah's hand, jerking her attention to the trees.

"Someone is out there."

Jay stood, following the boy's pointing finger.

A figure flickered between the trunks — too fast to see clearly.

A sound followed — not a horn, not a spirit, but the snap of someone stepping on a dead branch.

Jay's heart kicked.

"Stay behind me," he said.

He stepped forward, scanning the shadows.

Another movement.

Closer this time.

Someone was watching them.

Alive.

Breathing.

Afraid.

And judging by the way the spirit's frost lay thick in the bootprints trailing away from the pit…

Not alone.

Jay tightened his fists.

"Whoever dug here," he whispered, "is still on this ridge."

Sarah's breath shook.

"And the spirit is with him?"

Jay nodded once, his voice low and certain.

"Yes."

Chapter 25 When The Living Are Haunted

Ridge of Echoes — Moments Later

The forest held its breath.

Jay moved silently, surveying the timberline. He could feel it — not just the spirit but the unmistakable pressure of a living man's panic. Fear left a scent in the woods. Not one you could smell, but one the land itself reacted to.

And right now, the ridge was soaked in it.

Sarah kept David close behind her, one hand braced on his shoulder and the other holding the abandoned flashlight like a potential weapon.

"Jay?" she hissed.

"Do you see him?"

Jay didn't answer.

He didn't need to speak for the forest to hear him.

He took another slow step down the ridge.

A branch cracked.

Close.

Too close.

Jay pivoted sharply toward a clump of low pines — and there he saw it:

A man hunkered behind the brush.

Breathing hard.

Dirt smeared across his jacket and jeans.

A backpack half-zipped and bulging with something large.

And behind him — the air chilled again.

Cold licked at Jay's skin like a warning hand.

The spirit was with him.

Jay raised one hand in a gesture he'd made a hundred times as a cop.

"Don't move," he said calmly. "You're not in trouble yet. Just stand up and show me your hands."

The man flinched, startled by Jay's voice.

He stumbled halfway to his knees — eyes wide, pupils blown wide with panic.

"Stay back," he rasped. "I'm not— I wasn't stealing anything! I didn't do anything wrong!"

Jay exhaled slowly.

Guilt was written all over him — in his posture, his trembling voice, the way he clutched his backpack as if it were a lifeline.

Sarah moved slightly to the side, keeping David behind her.

Jay kept his voice even.

"What's your name?"

The man wiped mud from his forehead with shaking fingers.

"Mark," he whispered. "Mark Halverson."

Jay's stomach clenched — he recognized the name.

Local.

Trouble from time to time.

The kind of guy who chased stories and artifacts he had no business touching.

Jay took a careful step forward.

"Mark… did you dig up something on this ridge?"

Mark shook his head violently.

"No! No, I—"

But he broke off suddenly, his eyes darting to the shadows around him.

His breath quickened.

His hands trembled.

His pupils dilated with raw terror.

Jay followed his gaze.

A darker shape loomed between two trees.

Half-formed.

Unstable.

A ripple of sorrow and cold.

The spirit.

"Mark," Jay said slowly, "look at me. Not at it. Look at me."

Mark pressed a hand to his chest.

"I didn't mean to… I didn't know someone was buried there… I didn't know—"

Jay took one more step.

"What did you take?"

Mark swallowed hard, tears pricking his eyes.

"I—I thought it was just old carvings. Like a relic. Like what collectors buy. I thought— I thought it was nothing important!"

Jay clenched his jaw.

"You took something sacred."

Mark screamed and flailed back into a tree trunk, sliding halfway to the ground.

"I didn't know! I swear I didn't know! But when I was leaving—"

His voice broke.

"It started following me."

The spirit's outline shimmered, floating closer.

Sarah whispered, "Jay — it's attached to him."

Jay nodded.

"It feeds on guilt," Jay said softly. "On wounds people haven't faced. It saw his fear the moment he struck the shovel into the earth."

Mark covered his ears.

"Make it stop... please... I can't— I can't breathe—"

Jay raised both hands, voice level.

"Mark, listen to me. You need to put the item back. Whatever you took — it doesn't belong to you."

Mark shook his head wildly.

"I can't," he whispered, voice cracking. "If I go near that place again— it'll kill me."

Jay took a step closer.

"No. It's not here to kill. It's here because you broke something sacred. Spirits don't want revenge. They want balance."

Mark sobbed, hands shaking uncontrollably.

"I can't go back there… I can't…"

Behind him, the shadow twisted — growing, pulsing with his fear.

Sarah whispered urgently, "Jay… it's getting stronger."

Jay nodded slowly.

"I know."

He dropped to one knee a few feet from Mark, lowering his voice.

"Mark. You need to give me the backpack."

Mark clutched it tighter, shaking his head.

"No. No— you don't understand. If I let it go, it comes closer. It— it touched me. It touched me last night. In my truck. I couldn't breathe…"

Jay's stomach dropped.

The spirit had already begun sinking into him — like a weight, like a wound gnawing from the inside.

Jay reached out his hand.

"Mark… let me help you."

Mark looked at Jay's hand like it was a lifeline.

His lip trembled.

His breath shuddered.

Then — slowly — he loosened his grip and held out the backpack.

For a moment, everything was still.

But as soon as Jay touched the strap—

The forest dropped into silence.

The spirit lunged.

Not toward Mark.

Toward Jay.

A cold shock punched into Jay's chest.

Like grief.

Like every failure he'd ever buried.

Like the river dragging him back to places he couldn't fix.

Sarah screamed his name.

David sobbed.

Mark collapsed in the dirt.

Jay staggered back, fighting to keep his footing.

And the spirit whispered — not in words, but in weight:

You carry pain too.

You carry guilt too.

Let me in…

Jay clenched his fists and pushed back with a growl.

"No."

The shadow quivered — uncertain, frustrated — then drew back into the trees.

But not far.

Never far.

Jay knelt down, breath shaking, gripping the backpack like an anchor preventing him from collapsing.

Inside, something shifted — a carved object wrapped in cloth.

Old.

Powerful.

Out of place in the modern world.

Sarah rushed to Jay's side.

"Are you okay?"

Jay nodded weakly.

"It tried," he whispered. "It tried to attach to me too."

Mark lay on the ground sobbing.

"What do I do?" he begged. "Please… tell me what I do…"

Jay looked at the disturbed earth.

The frost.

The shattered peace of the ridge.

"You put it back," Jay said softly.

"You return what wasn't yours."

Sarah swallowed.

"And then?"

Jay looked toward the trees where the spirit waited — a shape carved from sorrow.

"Then," he murmured, "we pray the old ways and the new can both help it find its way home."

He stood slowly, the weight of two worlds settling on his shoulders.

"Because this isn't over."

www.ingramcontent.com/pod-product-compliance
Lightning Source LLC
Chambersburg PA
CBHW071418300726
48976CB00004B/1168

9 781970 577242